1

Table of Contents

Chapter 1 – Hemingway House

"Do you think I could get a pool like that?" Amy joked.

Heather laughed. She and her friends and family had decided to visit the Hemingway House as their weekend Key West outing. They had taken a guided tour around the premises and had just heard about how difficult installing and maintain this luxury pool had been in the 1930s.

The guide had also told them a story about how Ernest Hemingway had gotten exasperated with the cost of the undertaking and had flung a penny onto the patio, telling his wife that she had spent everything except his last penny on the project and so she might as well have it too. As a tribute to the tale, a penny was embedded in the cement at the north end of the pool.

"I'd give you my last penny to build it too," said Amy.

"I think he might have had more pennies that you did, Ames. This cost $20,000 to build, and that was in the 1930s."

The friends laughed and continued exploring the grounds and looking at the lush gardens with the rest of their group. The group included Heather's husband, Ryan, and Amy's boyfriend, Jamie, who were enjoying learning about how Hemingway used to have a boxing ring and would spar with local amateur fighters. Their senior friends Eva and Leila were still talking about how they enjoyed seeing the house and what the famous writer's décor looked like inside. They were big fans of his chandeliers.

Heather's twelve-year-old daughter, Lilly, appeared at alongside her mom.

"Are you feeling inspired?" Heather asked her.

"To build a pool?" Amy asked, continuing with her joke. "I know where we can get some shovels if you want to start digging."

"I meant inspired creatively," said Heather. "Lilly writes amazing dinosaur detective stories, and I wondered if being in a famous writer's house was giving her any new ideas."

Lilly shrugged. "I get ideas from all sorts of things, but I never know when inspiration will strike."

"I think your mother would prefer that the basis for your first book doesn't come from getting wounded in a war like Hemingway," said Amy.

"I knew his name before, and I'm learning a lot about him today," Lilly said. "But I feel bad that I didn't know much about him before."

"He wrote several classics in American literature," said Heather. "Like *A Farewell to Arms, For Whom the Bell Tolls,* and *The Old Man and the Sea*. But I don't think they are things that you would read until you're in high school."

"I know *A Farewell to Arms* has to be about war, but it did give me a different sort of idea about tiny T-Rex arms. I bet that could be a clue in a dinosaur mystery. He wouldn't be able to pick something up."

"Inspiration really can strike anywhere!" Amy said.

"We're going to have a very literary weekend," said Heather. "Hemingway House for our family outing and tomorrow is Bernadette's Mystery Writer Panel."

"Are you prepared with the donuts for it?" Amy asked.

"Am I ever not prepared with donuts?" Heather teased. "Yes. I have a perfect tropical flavor for it. You can all get a sample of it tonight, and we'll bake and deliver them to Bernadette's bookshop tomorrow."

"Think about it," Amy said to Lilly. "If you become a famous writer, you could get invited to panels all over the world too. To places with nice beaches like here. Or places with other nice things to see too. Like the Eiffel Tower or snow."

Lilly giggled. "That would be cool. Right now, I'm just writing for fun though. And because it gives me something to do when I miss my best friend."

"I know Nicolas misses you just as much," said Heather. "And we'll make sure he visits for spring break."

Lilly nodded and then said, "Can I go and look at the cats?"

"There are cats here?" Amy asked.

"Hemingway cats," Heather said. "They're known for having six toes on their feet."

"I don't want to make Dave and Cupcake jealous," Lilly said, referring to their pets at home. "But I'd like to see the polydactyl cats."

"Go right ahead." Heather nodded. "We'll be right behind you."

Lilly skipped off towards where she saw a cat. She must have told Eva and Leila about them too because they joined her in the kitty search. Heather and Amy followed behind at a slower pace so they could talk.

"If she's using words like polydactyl, then she must be a good writer," Amy said.

"She writes great stories. And I'm not just saying that because I'm her mom. She has some very clever ideas. However, I'm afraid that's she's been writing more because she hasn't made any good friends since we moved here. She's friendly with several people, but she hasn't found a new best friend. And it's not that I want to replace Nicolas. I want them to remain friends. But he's still in Texas, and I think she needs someone closer to talk to."

"Just invite some kids over one day. Between Lilly's personality and your donuts, she'll be sure to make friends."

"She's been hesitant to do so," said Heather.

"Well, she'll figure it out. She's a smart kid."

"And on the plus side, I can bring her to the mystery panel tomorrow. Bernadette said that the spy writer's stories might be a little scary, but there shouldn't be anything inappropriate at the panel discussion."

"Bernadette's Beachy Books isn't a huge store. How are they going to fit a huge panel discussion inside?"

"She told me that the authors are going to take turns at one table throughout the day to sign books. Then, the panel discussion that night is going to have a small live audience. Only about thirty people."

"So, we should be honored that our whole group is invited to come?"

"It's nice to be friends with the store owner," Heather agreed. "The discussion is going to be recorded and set up as a podcast so others, who can't be at the event, can still listen to it."

"I don't know what I'm more excited for. Meeting the famous mystery writers or trying your new tropical donuts."

"I think I'm excited to see some of these six-toed cats before I need to go to Donut Delights and start baking."

"Just don't cross paths with any black cats," said Amy with a laugh. "We don't need any bad luck if we're going to be dealing

with people who plot out murders
for a living."

Chapter 2 – Mystery Donuts

"They smell delicious," Janae said.

"Yes," said Nina. "What flavor is this?"

Heather grinned at her assistants mischievously. Her four employees and Amy were gathered around the Donut Delights kitchen counter where Heather had just unveiled her newest creation.

"This is the flavor I created that we will serve at Bernadette's Beachy Books today, but because it's for a Mystery Writers' Convention, I thought I'd carry that theme through with the donuts."

"Do they contain clues?" Digby asked. "Are they murder weapons? Are they poisoned?"

"If she poisoned her whole staff, then she wouldn't have anyone to work the front counter," Amy joked.

"I just meant that I would keep the donut's name a mystery until after you all tried it," said Heather. "I thought you could guess what the flavor was."

"I like that game a lot better than what I was thinking," Digby said, grabbing a donut.

The other assistants followed suit, examining theirs as they picked it up. It was yellow and white with a creamy-looking frosting on top.

Nina was biting her lip as she looked at the donut, nervous about guessing wrong. Janae pushed her beautiful red hair away from her face and began to smell her sample. Maternal Luz was focusing on the cream on top.

"Could it be a lemon meringue?" Luz wondered.

"Maybe it's yellow because it's banana flavored?" suggested Nina.

"I can't place the smell yet," said Janae. "But I think it's a tropical fruit."

"You know the best way to get to the bottom of this?" Digby asked. Then, he took a big bite of his donut. It took him a moment to chew and swallow before he could speak his guess, "It's pineapple."

"I like the way he thinks," said Amy. She took a bite of her donut, and the others did too.

"Definitely pineapple," Janae agreed. "That's what the smell is."

"I like that the donut base is pineapple flavored," said Nina. "But it also has a pineapple center with real chunks of the fruit."

Heather nodded. "I used a special pineapple jelly center."

"The cream topping is superb," said Luz. "It's light, but I like that it's piled on, so there is a lot of it."

"You've done perfectly," Heather said. "This is the Pineapple Cream Donut."

"Good teamwork, everyone," Digby said. "I think I might have been the MVP though."

"It is a wonderful flavor," Luz said. "And even if these are for murder mystery writers, I'm glad you didn't decide to make them look like they were filled with blood or something like that."

"I decided to make a flavor that was more reminiscent of tropical Key West instead," said Heather. "Bernadette said that she is able to convince writers to come because it's like a vacation for them to be here."

"Key West's beaches, your donuts, and the chance to talk to fans and other writers? It sounds like a good deal for them to be a part of it," said Janae.

"I can't wait until I have fans," said Digby.

"Amy and I will bring this batch of the Pineapple Cream Donuts over to the bookshop now and make sure that Bernadette is doing okay," Heather said. "And then, we'll be back to bake some more. I think it will be a busy day in the kitchen."

"People who go to the bookstore down the street will most likely stop here too to try some of our other flavors," said Amy. "I know I would."

As they boxed up the finished Pineapple Cream Donuts for traveling, they started talking

about the event. Heather
promised that if they could keep
on schedule with all their baking,
there would be opportunities for
the employees to slip over to the
bookstore and get some
autographs.

Janae and Nina were planning on
going to the discussion that night.
Unfortunately, Digby had
rehearsal for his play, and Luz
already had a family obligation so
they couldn't attend the evening
event.

Janae followed Heather and Amy
to the front of the shop, while the
other employees began bringing
the rest of the day's donuts from
the kitchen to the display cases.

The duo was about to depart to the bookshop as Janae flipped the sign on the door from "closed" to "open," ready to deal with any early morning customers.

However, Janae wasn't quite ready to deal with the two customers who rushed inside the moment the door opened as if they had been lying in waiting.

"Bernadette can wait a minute, right?" asked Amy. "I want to see how this plays out."

"Fine," Heather said, admitting that she was a bit curious herself.

"Hi, Janae."

"How are you this fine morning?"

"I'm fine," Janae said. "Would you like a donut?"

The two customers looked at one another. Detective Peters and Fire Frank both had feelings for Janae and had been awkward about sharing this information with her. It looked as if they might both be working up the courage to tell her. Unfortunately, it might be at the same time.

"Janae, you know that I've always had a thing for you," Detective Peters said.

"Ever since I went on that bike ride with you, I've been smitten," said Fire Frank.

"And, well, being a detective - I think that being on top of a potential crime wave is important, and listening to crime writers discuss murders could be an invaluable resource," Detective Peters said, trying to sound impressive to cover up his nerves. "And so, I was wondering if you would like to attend the panel discussion with me, an officer of the law."

"Or if you'd like to go with a firefighter who is a huge fan of Patterson Blake, maybe you'd like to go with me?" said Fire

Frank with a slight blush.

"Because I'd love to go with you."

Janae looked back and forth
between the two men.

"I've had an inkling that you both
felt this way," she said.
"Unfortunately, I'm not quite sure
what my own feelings are. You
both seem like great guys, but I
don't really *know* either of you.
And you've been acting so
strange and competitive lately
when you came into the shop."

Both men seemed to deflate.

"We were trying to impress you,"
Detective Peters said, looking at

the ground. "In maybe not the best way."

"We were a little ridiculous with that push-up competition in the donut shop," Fire Frank agreed.

"I was planning on going to the discussion tonight. Would you be interested in all going together?" Janae suggested. "We could get to know each other as friends first."

"I think that would be nice," Fire Frank said.

"And we'll make sure not to be so competitive," Detective Peters agreed. "So you can get to know who we really are."

"I'd like that a lot," Janae said. "And here, let me get you both a donut."

Heather and Amy left the shop as Janae picked out some donuts for her friends.

"Do you think they'll be able to stop themselves from being competitive?" Amy asked.

"I don't know," Heather said. "I've been determined to refrain from being a matchmaker in this situation."

"I don't know if I'm Team Frank or Team Peters," Amy said.

Heather chuckled.

They walked down the street until they reached Bernadette's Beachy Books.

"I'm so glad you're here!" The bookseller exclaimed as they came in. "This event is killing me."

Chapter 3 – Panel Prep

"It's killing you?" Heather asked.

"Everything that could go wrong seems to be going wrong," Bernadette said. She pushed her glasses up her nose and sighed. "I feel like Jay Gatsby when his plan to win back Daisy wasn't going so well."

"Take a break from setting up," Heather suggested.

"And a break from the literary references," said Amy.

"And enjoy a Pineapple Cream Donut," said Heather, offering her friend one.

"Thank you," Bernadette said, taking a deep breath and accepting the snack. She took a bite and then smiled. "At least one thing is going right now. This is perfect. Thank you."

"Thank you for letting my whole big family come to the panel discussion tonight."

"I'm happy to," Bernadette said. "Besides, with how many mysteries you two solve, you probably have some tricks that you could teach them."

Heather laughed while Amy nodded as if it were the solemn truth. Bernadette happily finished her donut.

"Now," Heather said. "What's going wrong? And what can we help with?"

"The main problem is that my air conditioner broke," said Bernadette. "And I can't get someone to come until Monday afternoon. That means we won't have air conditioning all day for the event."

"Can we open the windows?"

"That's what I think I'm going to do. I normally don't like having them open because I wouldn't want anything from outside to damage the books. It's supposed to be clear weather today though. I might have lucked out there."

"It's not going to be a dark and stormy night for the mystery writers?" Amy teased.

"No," Bernadette said. "And that's good. I'm also having trouble setting up the equipment for recording the podcast. One of our connecting wires wasn't the right size. But my assistant Gina is taking care of that. It will be fixed in time."

"Those are certainly challenges, but it sounds like you're handling them well," Heather said, complimenting her friend.

"Now, if I could just handle the writers," said Bernadette.

"Bernadette!" a woman bellowed as she approached. She had hair pulled back in a tight bun and was carrying a cell phone that looked permanently attached to her hand.

"Which writer is this?" asked Amy.

"This is Jess Krueger," Bernadette explained. "She's the author Dennis Grimm's manager."

"And it's because I'm thinking of Dennis that I'm so upset," Jess Krueger said. "It's way too hot in here. Is it true the air conditioner isn't working?"

"I'm afraid not, but I'll open the windows fully, and I can install some fans if need be," Bernadette said.

Jess looked like she had more words to say on the matter, but her phone rang, and she walked away to answer it.

"Is everyone giving you such trouble?" asked Heather.

"Want us to direct them how to walk off the pier?" Amy asked.

"She's the most particular about things," said Bernadette. "As I said, she manages Dennis Grimm. He writes those werewolf detective books that are pretty popular right now."

"I've heard of him," Heather agreed.

"The authors haven't been too demanding," said Bernadette. "But they can be quirky. They should be filing in soon to make sure that everything is set before we begin."

As they waited for the authors to arrive, Bernadette told them more about her writers' event. She had been having one annually, alternating between different genres of books, in order to attract more business during a slow season. (It was right between when couples liked to travel to Key West for romantic Valentine's trips and when tourists arrived for spring break.) If the writers were big names, then customers would travel to get their books signed by the authors in person. A few customers could also stay for the live panel discussion.

It was a nice trip for the writers too. All they had to do was sit at a table and sign autographs for about an hour each, and then attend the talk that evening. Otherwise, they were free to soak in the sun, sand, and surf.

"That's Dennis Grimm," Bernadette said, indicating to a

young man with shaggy hair. "He's going to be signing autographs at the table first."

Dennis Grimm came up to them and shook their hands. "I hope Jess isn't giving you too much trouble. She just wants everything to be perfect for her clients."

"It's all right," Bernadette said. She went to show him where he would be at the table and where extra copies of his books stationed.

Heather and Amy decided to take the time to begin setting out their donuts. They started making a display on the snack table and made sure that lots of napkins were available so no one would pick up a book with sticky fingers.

"Enchanting looking donuts. I do hope that they aren't hiding any arsenic inside."

"Why is everyone convinced we're poisoning donuts today?" Amy asked.

"Apologies," the older man who approached them said. "It's a bad habit from the trade. Looking for murders everywhere."

"I recognize you from a book jacket cover picture," Heather said. "But I can't quite place the name."

"Art Sanford."

"Of course," said Heather. "You wrote some real classics."

"I was on the Best Sellers' List nearly every week in the seventies. It's been more difficult recently. But you can't deny that I was a master."

"We're excited to hear you talk on the panel tonight," Heather said.

"I'm rather excited about it myself. It's been too long since I was asked to speak anywhere. And I'm glad you'll be here. It's right to have an audience," he said with a smile. "I have a surprise for tonight. A surprise to die for."

Heather and Amy exchanged a look. They hoped he was joking.

Chapter 4 – The Surprise

It was a busy day, but Heather had a lot of fun. Her Pineapple Cream Donuts were a huge success at the signings and customers were flocking over to Donut Delights to try their other flavors. Even as her donuts were flying off their shelves, her team was able to keep up a steady stream of baking.

She was covered in sugar and icing when they closed up shop for the day, but she was in good spirits. She had also kept her promise that her employees could get autographs through the day, and Luz was ecstatic that she had gotten a signed copy of an Art Sandford book.

After changing into something less floury to wear to the evening event, Heather recruited her family to help her bring the donuts over to the bookshop.

"You seem calmer than before," Heather said to Bernadette, as they walked in.

"We survived the book signings today, and Gina got the equipment working to record the podcast. With you arriving with the donuts, the final piece of the puzzle is in place."

Heather reset the donut display with some help from Lilly and Ryan. Then, they decided which seats they should take, opting for a section in the front by an open window where there might be a breeze.

Amy and Jamie soon joined them. Jamie was carrying his copy of Patterson Blake's new book that he had gotten signed that afternoon. He had rewrapped it in bubble wrap to protect the precious item.

Eva and Leila arrived, along with Eva's beau Vincent who was sporting a bowtie with pictures of magnifying glasses on it. They were all excited to hear what Art Sandford would say. He had been out of the limelight for a while, but they were still fans of his.

Heather looked around to see her assistants arriving. Nina blushed as she passed the young man who was working at the neighboring shop Sun and Fun Novelties and sat on the opposite side of the room. Janae entered with Fire Frank and Detective Peters. Maybe her plan of being friends was working because the two men didn't seem to be competing. They were exceptionally cordial to one another as they took their seats.

Gina and Bernadette were putting the final touches on setting up the room, and the audience knew that the writers would soon be coming out to begin.

"Who are you most excited to see, Lilly?" Heather asked.

"I don't know them very well, so maybe Lori Laurels because she's a lady writer. I think it will be interesting to hear everyone though."

Ryan's phone rang, and he answered it quickly. A resigned look came over this face as the conversation progressed.

When he hung up, he turned to Heather and said, "Looks like a detective's work is never done."

"Do you have a new case?"

"Possibly," said Ryan. "There have been reports of a dead body on the other side of the island that I need to go check out."

"Do you want Amy and I to come with you?" Heather asked. Since becoming private investigators, she and her bestie had helped him with many cases.

Ryan shook his head. "I'll check it out on my own. You two can join me later if it looks like a tough case. But until then, you can stay with Lilly. She's excited about this."

Heather nodded and gave him a kiss goodbye. Ryan scanned the crowd for his partner and then told Detective Peters that they needed to go. Peters looked miserable as he left Janae with Fire Frank, but he did his duty and left to investigate the call.

Heather was disappointed that Ryan got called away and was so wrapped in her own thoughts that she didn't realize that Amy and Jamie were bickering.

"Stop popping the bubble wrap," Amy said.

"I can't help it," said Jamie. "I know I got it to protect the book, but now I can't stop popping."

Amy grabbed the bubble wrap and threw it out the open window.

49

"That's littering," said Jamie. "Ryan could arrest you for that."

"Ryan's not here," said Amy. "And we can pick it up after the panel. But I don't want you popping during their answers."

It was good timing because a moment later, Bernadette came out to greet the crowd.

"Good evening, everyone! It's no mystery why you're here. After a wonderful day of book signings, we are going to have our talented mystery writers discuss how they come up with their exciting book ideas. And we're going to record this discussion, and it will be available to re-listen to later this week. But without further ado, let me introduce our writers."

She began by introducing Art Sandford. He had the same roguish look on his face that he had when they met him at the donut table. He took his seat at the end of the row of chairs and was closest to Heather.

Next came Patterson Blake, a spy thriller writer, who was dressed like he was incognito himself. He was wearing an all-black outfit and dark glasses even though they were inside.

"He does know that they're just recording their voices, right?"

said Amy. "His face isn't going to be seen on camera."

Heather contained a chuckle and shushed her friend. She wasn't sure how sensitive the recording equipment was, but she didn't want their audience comments to end up on the podcast.

The next writer was Lori Laurels. She had stylish dark hair and wore bright colors. Her mysteries sounded they included a lot of romance. As Heather listened to the racy titles of her books, she suspected that they had a lot of steamy scenes in them, and she was glad that Lilly hadn't actually read them.

Finally came the youngest writer, Dennis Grimm. His shaggy hair seemed fitting for his werewolf detective series.

They took their seats and Bernadette began asking them about their creative processes. As the discussion progressed, it was interesting to hear how the writers differed. Patterson Blake was a bit closed mouth in his answers but said that he liked to let real life inspire him. Lori Laurels said that she liked to imagine the most romantic places for couples to meet and then plan a murder at the site so their romance would have complications. Dennis Grimm explained how he was interested in duality with his wolf character and so he always felt like he was planning two stories at the same time.

Art Sandford simply said that he liked to begin with a red herring or a misled. He had a huge smile on his face when the lights went out.

Chapter 5 – Darkness

"Is this part of the show?" Amy asked.

"I don't know," Heather said, holding Lilly close to her.

Heather heard Bernadette groan and suspected that this was something else that was going wrong. Who had turned off the lights? And why?

"Just stay calm," Heather said, trying to get her eyes to adjust to the darkness.

Suddenly there was a loud bang.

"How can this be?" said a man's voice. "Here?"

"What was that?" Janae cried out.

It was followed by another bang, and this time Heather recognized the sound. It was a gunshot. Someone screamed.

"I don't know if I can stay calm anymore," Amy said.

"I wish I could see," said Jamie.

Heather wished the same thing, but she knew she couldn't just sit in the dark any longer. She rose to action and led Lilly so that she was closer to Amy and Jamie.

"Lilly, stay with Aunt Amy," Heather said. "And stay low."

Heather took out her keychain. She had a tiny flashlight dangling on it and used the light to work her way through the crowd that was starting to panic. She found the light switch and turned it on.

There was a collective sigh of relief as the light returned, but it soon turned to horror again. Art Sandford was slumped in his chair with blood staining his shirt. He was obviously dead.

Heather looked around the room. Was everyone here a suspect?

Fire Frank rose to his feet, though Janae was still holding tightly onto him.

"I'm with the Fire Department," he said. "I'm going to call the police and tell them that they need to get over here right away. I need everyone to stay calm and to stay near the building until they arrive."

"What if we're still in danger?" a woman who looked similar to Lori Laurels asked.

"The shooting has stopped, and the police are going to want to question us all," said Fire Frank.

Heather suddenly felt exhausted. She headed back to where her friends were sitting and hugged her daughter. She thought Fire Frank was doing a fine job containing the scene and she would let him handle it. She needed to make sure that Lilly felt safe.

***

"This is terrible," Chief Chet said. "A prominent writer was killed in our town, and I can't remember the last time that I was the first responder on a case."

"Ryan and Peters will be here as soon as they can," said Heather. "The other call put them on the other side of the island."

"I know. And I'm happy to do my part. I just hate having to deal with dead bodies," the chief said.

"Look, Chief," Heather said. "I know that you're going to have to question everyone that was here tonight."

"Exactly. That's an awful lot of work to do. But it will have to be done. It had to be somebody here who killed him."

"Yes. And I understand that you have to question everyone, but I'd like to get Lilly out of here."

"Oh, yes. Of course. We can't have a twelve-year-old at a crime scene."

"Thank you," Heather said. "Now I'll just have to figure out where is best for her. Most of the people who I would ask to babysit are already here."

"She can go to my house," Chief Chet said. "I'll have my wife swing by here. My daughter Chelsea is about her age. And it will get her away from the murder."

Heather thanked him, pleased that one aspect of the problem had been solved. Fire Frank had moved the writers and audience outside where they were waiting for be questioned. The bookstore was getting roped off with caution tape until the medical examiner could collect the body.

Jess Krueger walked over to the group.

"What's going on?" she asked. "What happened to the panel discussion?"

"Jess, it's so terrible," Dennis said. "Art Sandford was killed."

"This is a joke, right?"

"Does it look like I'm joking?" he asked.

"How could this happen?"

"That's what we're going to have to find out, ma'am," Chief Chet said.

"Why weren't you at the panel discussion?" Heather asked, realizing that she hadn't seen the manager inside the bookshop that evening.

"I was running late because I had an important call with a publisher. I thought the panel would still be going on."

"We all did," Amy added, joining them.

Jess Krueger frowned and then walked away with her client. Heather was frowning too, but she felt some relief when Chief Chet's wife arrived. Heather hugged Lilly and assured her that they would figure everything out.

"I'm sure you will, Mom. You're great at solving mysteries. I just wish I wasn't here when such a scary one started."

"I love you," Heather said.

"I love you too."

Mrs. Copeland chimed in and said, "I know this isn't the ideal situation, but we'd meant to invite you over. I'm sure you and Chelsea will have a nice time. And I'll make hot cocoa when we get home."

Heather thanked her and watched them leave. After making sure that Lilly was okay,

Heather shifted her attention to checking on Bernadette.

"I just can't believe this happened," Bernadette said. "When I had a romance writers panel, there wasn't spontaneously a wedding."

"We're going to get to the bottom of this," said Heather.

Bernadette shook her head. "I was trying to increase business with a nice creative event, but now my shop is going to be forever known as the place where Art Sandford was killed."

"Maybe that could be a selling point?" Amy suggested. "Like the places people go because they think it's haunted."

Bernadette looked like she might burst into tears.

"Don't worry," Heather said, pointing. "Look. Ryan and Detective Peters are here."

Bernadette nodded as Heather tried once more to reassure her. Then, she went over to meet the detectives. After telling Ryan that Lilly was taken care of, she asked about his other case.

"It wasn't a dead body," Ryan said. "It was just some discolored driftwood caught in seaweed."

"Then talk about bad timing," Amy said.

"Definitely," Peters agreed. Though whether he was talking about the murder or his friendly date being interrupted, they didn't know.

"Peters and I will have to take initial statements from everyone," said Ryan, surveying the scene. "But first I'd like to check with the medical examiner."
Heather nodded and followed him back inside the bookshop. Amy groaned, unenthusiastic about returning to where there was actually a dead body.

Ryan greeted the medical examiner, a small, frail man with big eyes.

"What can you tell me so far, Rudy?"

"It's an unusual murder. Very strange."

"You mean besides the fact that it took place in a room full of people?" asked Amy. "Some of whom were famous mystery writers?"

"How is it strange?" asked Ryan.

"Well, you see this blood on the front of his shirt?" the medical examiner asked.

Amy turned away so she wouldn't have to see it. However, Heather braced herself and took a step forward to join Ryan and Peters and examine the dead body.

"This blood on the front of his shirt is fake."

"Fake?" asked Peters.

The medical examiner nodded. "Like the stuff used for costumes. However, the blood and gunshot wound on his back is very real." "That is strange," Ryan said, agreeing with the earlier assessment and scratching his head.

"What sort of a killer are we dealing with?" asked Heather.

Chapter 6 – Station Talk

After a restless night, Heather
and Amy joined Ryan and
Detective Peters at the police
station in the morning. None of
them were feeling especially
cheerful, but the Pineapple
Cream Donuts that Heather
brought were making the morning
more manageable.

"There really should have been a
warning that this could have
happened on the event flyers,"
Amy joked.

Heather couldn't bring herself to
laugh. "Murders are always
terrible. And, of course, I'm very
upset for poor Art Sandford.
However, I'm also furious that

this happened when Lilly was there."

"We couldn't have known this would happen when we decided to bring her," Ryan said.

"I don't blame us. I blame the murderer," Heather said. "He killed a famous writer. He committed the crime in a room where a child was. And he's hurting my friend's business."

"It was a terrible night all around," said Detective Peters.

Heather sighed. "I need to stay calm and look at this objectively, but it's more difficult than usual. Knowing that Lilly could have been in danger. However, I'll use the feelings as fuel to do my best work on this case. Because I want to catch this bad guy more than ever."

"I hate to be the one to bring this up, but is it possible that the person we should be mad at is Art Sandford?" asked Amy.

"You mean that he killed himself?" asked Ryan.

"He did mention to us that he had a surprise for the event," said Amy. "Something to die for."

"He was up to something," Heather admitted.

"Maybe he was planning on killing himself," Amy said, thinking aloud. "He was sick, or he owed too many people money. There could be reasons for it. And he decided that he wanted to do it dramatically. Go out with a bang, sort to speak."

"And he used the fake blood to cause confusion?" asked Heather.

Amy nodded. "Yeah. He was trying to create a mysterious story even after his death. It would maintain an air of mystery around him and turn him into a legend."

"It makes as much sense as anything else right now," Heather said.

"I did a little research on Art Sandford this morning," Detective Peters said. "I didn't find any obvious red flags for enemies. He had been out of the news for a little while. He hadn't had a successful book in a few years. However, there was something interesting."

"What?" asked Heather.

"He did have a gun registered in his name. It's from about ten years ago, but it's the same caliber as the what the medical examiner found in his preliminary findings."

"It all fits!" said Amy.

"Of course, he might have had a hard time shooting himself in the back," Ryan pointed out.

Amy grumbled and admitted he was right. The gears in Heather's mind were turning. If Art Sandford really had wanted to kill himself dramatically in front of an audience, then he might have plotted out the perfect way to do it. He could have figured out a device to cause the fatal blow and keep them all guessing about it.

However, would Art Sandford have wanted to kill himself? He seemed so happy about being a part of the panel discussion. He seemed excited to be recognized for his writing work. He did tell them that he had a surprise planned. However, Heather expected it to be something more along the lines of announcing a new book than a dramatic suicide.

If he didn't kill himself, then who killed him? Was it one of the other writers? What motive did they have?

She chewed on a Pineapple Cream Donut as she chewed on the problem. Chief Chet must have smelled the donuts and joined the group.

"How is the case progressing?" he asked.

"We've still got a lot of work to do," Ryan admitted.

"I'm confident you'll all figure it out," Chief Chet said, selecting a donut. "And I think Lilly had a good time with Chelsea last night."

"It's a shame it had to happen under such horrible circumstances," said Heather.

They were interrupted in their discussion by the arrival of a newcomer. Heather recognized the young man as someone who had been at the writers' panel the night before.

He looked like he hadn't gotten any sleep during the night. He was sweating and rubbing his hands together.

"Can I help you?" Ryan asked.

The young man sighed. "I've been thinking about this all night. I decided I can't hide from it anymore. I've got to turn myself in. I'd like to talk to the detectives in charge of Art Sandford's murder."

"That's us," said Ryan.

"I've come here to confess."

Chapter 7 – The Confession

Ryan and Detective Peters led
the young man into the
interrogation room. They were
making sure that he understood
his rights and agreed to waive
counsel willingly.

Chief Chet chomped on a donut.
"Just when you thought you were
stumped, you get a break like
this. You guys are lucky."

After everything that happened,
Heather wasn't feeling very lucky,
but she kept her comments to
herself. She faced the two-way
mirror to watch the detectives
record the man's confession.

"I wish they'd all confess like this," Amy said. "It would make our jobs easier."

"Let's not get ahead of ourselves yet," said Heather. "Let's hear what he has to say."

They watched as Ryan and Peters began their questions.

"What's your name for the record?" asked Peters.

"Connor Johnson."

"And what was your relationship to Art Sandford?"

"I was his assistant. I was relatively new. I've only been

working for him for a few months. I thought it was because he hadn't had a new book in a while, so he didn't need an assistant. Not until he signed up for the podcast and book signing. I thought he needed someone to help with his travel arrangements. And at first, his idea for the panel discussion seemed harmless. Of course, now I see how it all really is."

"And how is it really?" Detective Peters asked, confused.

"He hired me as an assistant because he wanted somebody who didn't know him well. Somebody who wouldn't understand what he was up to."

"What was he up to?" prompted
Ryan.

"His murder."

Ryan and Peters exchanged a
look.

"Are you suggesting that Art
Sandford killed himself?" asked
Ryan.

"That has to be it," Connor said.
"And I knew that sooner or later
you'd connect me to it, so I
thought it was better just to come
clean about it now. But I need
you to understand that I didn't
know about his real plan. I only
knew the fake plan. And I didn't
want you to think I was more

involved than I was because I wasn't."

"Are you confused?" Amy asked her friend.

However, Heather was already headed to the entrance of the interrogation room. She knocked on the door, and Ryan admitted her. Amy followed right behind her.

"These are some private investigators who assist us on difficult matters," Ryan explained as the women sat down.

"And this seems to be a difficult matter," Amy muttered. "Not the confession that we thought it was."

"Mr. Johnson, did you have anything to do with Art Sandford's death?" Heather asked, deciding to be blunt.

"No," Connor said quickly. "Well, yes. But really no."

"Maybe you better start at the beginning?" Peters suggested.

Connor Johnson looked around the interrogation room and took a deep breath. "I started working as Art Sandford's assistant a few months ago when he agreed to come to this event here. Honestly, it seemed like a dream

come true. I was working for a
famous writer. We were going to
come to Key West for a book
signing. Everything seemed
great. And like I said, I thought
his idea seemed harmless. Funny
even."

"He mentioned to us that he had
a surprise," Heather said.

"And it ended up being a big
one," said Connor. "That wasn't
what he told me it would be."

"What did he tell you?" asked
Ryan.

"He said that he was going to
orchestrate a fake crime during
the podcast. He thought it would

be a great idea to build enthusiasm for his work again so that he would be able to publish a new novel. He was going to pretend to be murdered, and the other writers were going to have to solve it."

"Did Bernadette know about this?" asked Heather.

"The bookstore lady? No. Art Sandford was afraid that she might try and stop him. He wanted to prove that it would be hard to solve his murder."

"He succeeded," Amy said.

"He left clues in the room and wanted the other writers to figure out what happened. However, he wanted it to be difficult. He wanted to prove that he was the master crime writer."

"It sounds more and more like he did kill himself," Ryan said slowly.

"I was the one who turned out the lights and who made the first gunshot noise. I had the sound effect on my phone and was supposed to play it at the proper time. Red Herring was the code word for me to begin. I even had lines. I shouted out *how can this be*? But then everything went off script."

"You only fired one shot?" Heather asked.

"That's right," said Connor. "Art Sandford must have made the second shot go off. It scared me so much that I didn't turn the lights back on right away. I hid behind a chair."

"Do you know if Art Sandford brought his gun with him here?" asked Detective Peters.

"I don't know. I didn't know he had a gun. But he was keeping me in the dark about a lot of things. I really didn't know this was his plan."

"And you came here to talk to us just to assure us that you didn't kill your boss?" asked Amy.

"I bought the fake blood when we arrived on the island. We didn't want to have it in our suitcases when we flew in."

"If you flew in that would make traveling with the gun more difficult," said Peters. "But if Art Sandford had been planning this for months, he could have figured out a way to get it here."

"I figured you'd trace the blood back to me," Connor said. "I wanted you to know that I wasn't an accomplice to murder. I was just a dumb kid who accepted a job that was too good to be true."

"Mr. Johnson, if this wasn't by Art Sandford's own hand, do you know anyone who would want to hurt him?" Heather asked.

"I guess he and Patterson Blake didn't get along too well. Art Sandford said they had a past, and that he didn't really want to sit next to him at the panel. But there was a contract thing about Dennis Grimm being introduced last, so Art Sandford and Patterson Blake ended up next to each other. I guess being last makes Grimm sound more impressive," said Connor. "But you don't think someone else could have done this, do you? Art Sandford had planned everything out."

"I think we're going to have to return to the scene of the crime to see," Heather said.

Chapter 8 – The Crime Scene

"It makes me sad to see Bernadette's Beachy Books as a crime scene," Heather said.

"Me too," Amy agreed. "And I keep thinking about bad jokes to add to the alliteration in the name like Books and Bodies."

The two friends followed the detectives through the crime scene tape and into the bookshop. Donuts from the night before were still sitting on the food table. The recording equipment for the podcast was still set up. Chairs were moved into disorder from when the audience was panicking, and there was blood on the one

where Art Sandford had been
sitting.

It was strange to see a place they
knew so transformed. It had been
exciting to see it set up for the
writers' event, and terrible to see
the changes that the crime had
wrought upon the room.

Heather tried to contain her
emotions and look at the crime
scene objectively. They needed
to determine what was a part of
Art Sandford's plan for the night,
and if anything had deviated from
it.

"We know for sure that the first
gunshot and the fake blood were
part of Art Sandford's plan

because of Connor," Heather said, thinking aloud. "What else was a part of it?"

They all looked around the room, but Heather was the first to discover the sealed envelopes under the writers' chairs.

"What are they?" Amy asked.

"Clues," said Heather.

"Well, yeah. I know that."

"No," Heather said. "They're labeled as clues."

With gloved hands, they removed the envelopes from the bottom of the chairs and brought them over to the counter to examine them. Heather looked at the handwriting on the envelopes.

"Is there one of Art Sandford's signed books around?"

Peters looked around and found one. They compared both handwriting samples.

"I think it's a match," said Ryan.

"So that means that Art Sandford wrote these clues?" asked Amy. "Why?"

They looked inside the envelopes for an answer. Each one contained a character description. The one under Art

Sandford's chair labeled him as the victim and described him as a wealthy industrialist. The one that was under Patterson Blake's labeled him as a suspect. It also said that he was the industrialist's brother who would inherit the family business after the victim's death. Lori Laurel was also listed a suspect and was described as the wife of the industrialist. Dennis Grimm was the butler.

The letters went on to describe where everyone was at the time of the murder and whether they were right or left handed.

"It looks as if he plotted out the murder of this industrialist and wanted everyone to use the clues to determine who the killer was," said Heather. "Just like he told Connor Johnson he was doing."

"And then he added a real murder on top of it?" asked Amy. "Sounds like double kill."

"It does seem strange to me that he would go through all the trouble of planting these clues to solve the industrialist's murder and then do something that would cause everyone to run away in fear instead of sticking around to solve his game," said Heather.

"Could there be some sort of code in these clues?" asked Peters.

"Maybe," said Amy. "But Dennis Grimm isn't a butler in real life. And Lori Laurels and Art Sandford weren't married."

"And why would Art Sandford want us to solve a murder if the answer was that he killed himself?" Heather pondered.

"There's something else here that's important," Ryan said. "Or rather, something that isn't here."

"What?" asked Amy.

"There's no shooting device set up," Ryan explained. "There's no way that Art Sandford could have shot himself in the back at that angle with his own hand. If he were planning to kill himself, he would have needed to set up some sort of device that could shoot him in the proper way. I don't see anything like that here."

"There was a lot of chaos at the time," said Heather. "But Fire Frank was good at controlling the crowd once the lights were on, and I didn't see anyone tampering with potential evidence then."

"But if he didn't shoot himself," Amy said. "That means that somebody else did."

"And that means this was a murder," said Heather.

Ryan started tracking where the trajectory of the bullet would have to come from in order to hit the victim where it did.

"I think it had to come from the right side of the room," Ryan said finally.

"That's near where we were sitting," Heather said.

"Who else was near you after we left?" Ryan asked.

"The right side of the room ended up being the Key West crowd and the reserved seats for the writers' guests," Heather said, remembering. "The other side of the room was where the people who came to visit specifically for this event sat."

"Some vacation," said Amy.

"It was our group of friends near the front," said Heather. "And I'm trying to remember who was there as guests of the writers. I can't think of where Connor Johnson was."

"If he were preparing to turn off the lights, he wouldn't have been sitting by us," said Amy.
"There was a woman who looked like Lori Laurels in the audience near us," Heather continued.
"Maybe they're related?"

"Anyone else near you?" asked Ryan.

"We were a large group," said Heather. "We took up much of the front section."

"Of course, if someone were plotting a murder, he could have moved to the proper spot to shoot him," Detective Peters said. "Even if it was dark."

"So, one of the other writers could have done it," said Heather.

"In fact, it seems most likely," said Ryan. "It would have to be someone seated near you or someone who didn't have far to travel in the dark like the writers sitting next to Art Sandford."

"Great," Amy said. "They're all experts at plotting murders in their books. How do we figure out which one did it for real?"

They heard a noise outside, and all froze.

"Someone is here," Heather whispered. "Is it the killer coming back?"

Chapter 9 – A Serious Writer

Ryan and Detective Peters ventured out of the bookshop first, ready to draw their weapons if need be. Heather and Amy followed behind.

"I just wanted to listen to the writers talk about their books," Amy said. "I didn't want to enact one of their thrillers out."

They rounded the side of the building and saw someone testing the back-door entrance.

"Stop right there!" Ryan called out.

The woman stood up straight and greeted them with a sheepish smile.

"You caught me," Lori Laurels said, brushing her dark hair out of her face.

"Returning to the scene of the crime to collect some evidence you left behind?" Heather asked.

"Not me," Lori Laurels said. "To find what the killer left behind."

"Could be one and the same," said Amy.

"No, no," Lori said. "I'm here to help. I'm going to solve this crime."

"Ms. Laurels, we can appreciate your enthusiasm," Ryan said. "But this is a police matter."

"And we already have as much help as we need," Detective Peters said with a smile at the private investigators.

"We can't have you interfering with our investigation," said Ryan.

"You're not taking me seriously, are you? You're just like everyone else," Lori cried. "I am a legitimate writer. I plot wonderful mysteries with lots of twists. People try to delegitimize me by saying I only write bedroom scenes, but that's not true. I craft murders."

"I'm not sure she's helping her
case here," Amy said.

"I could be a real help to you,"
Lori continued. "I notice things.
Just like the heroines in my
books! And not just things like
how heavily muscled men can be
in the right ways, but clues. And I
bet I can find something helpful at
the scene. I've already begun
examining the door to see if the
killer could have entered this
way."

"They couldn't," said Heather. "Or
not without an accomplice and a
way to see in the dark. The door
is kept locked so no one can
sneak into the store and it leads
into the storage room that I know

Bernadette keeps stacked with books. It would be hard to maneuver in the dark."

Lori looked annoyed. "All right, so one thought I had didn't pan out. That doesn't mean that I can't help with the investigation."

"We can't allow that," Ryan began.

"But I am a serious mystery writer. If you let me prove that I could solve a real crime, then people would start taking me more seriously."

"What I mean to say," Ryan continued. "Is that we can't have anyone who could be considered a suspect in the murder case interfering with it."

"I'm a suspect?" Lori Laurels asked. "I suppose people might take me more seriously if they think that I might be a killer, but I didn't do anything. Why would you suspect me?"

"Because you're so great at plotting murders," Amy said, wryly.

Lori smiled. "I really am. And adding some steamy romance only enhances the plot."

Heather decided not to comment on that. Instead, she focused on the case. "Did you have a guest in the audience at the panel discussion?"

"Yes. My sister, Lana, was there. Why?"

"We're just trying to account for everyone," said Ryan.

"How well did you know Art Sandford?" Detective Peters asked, taking out his notebook.

"We went on a few dates before," Lori said. "But I still didn't know him that well. I realized he was too old for me. I didn't understand all the references he would make. And I felt like he didn't respect me as an author."

"That seems like the sort of thing that makes you mad," Heather commented.

"It sure does," said Lori. "And that's why I broke up with him. I need someone who respects me and my work."

"Ms. Laurels, how much did you know about Art Sandford's plan for that evening?" asked Ryan.

"What do you mean?"

"If you had dated, he might have felt close enough to share his idea for the night."

"I did get the sense that he was up to something," said Lori. "But he didn't tell me what. He had a smirk on his face all night though. I used to hate when he did that."

"It seems that he was plotting a crime," Ryan began.

"You can't think that Art did this to himself," Lori said. "He wouldn't have done that. He loved himself too much. And he was excited about being part of the panel discussion. He thought it meant that his career was going to take off again."

"Did he ever tell you about a story idea he might have had about an industrialist?" asked Heather.

"No, I don't think so. When we dated, he hadn't been writing for a while. He would only talk about old books. Maybe that was why he didn't like my books. It wasn't a reflection on them. It was that he was jealous that he couldn't come up with any good murders anymore."

"Do you know if Art Sandford had a gun?" asked Detective Peters.

Lori shook her head. "I don't know."

Heather had something else that she was curious about and asked, "Ms. Laurels, where were you when the shots fired?"

"I was in my seat at the front of the room. And then I ducked behind it. I was scared that someone was trying to kill us because we were famous. Crazed fans or something like that."

"Did you notice if anyone else was moving around you?"

"I don't think so. But I was terrified at the time. I might not have noticed," Lori said. "But in general, I am really good at noticing things."

"Thank you for your help," Ryan said.

"We'll make sure to take what you said seriously," said Heather.

Chapter 10 – Assistants' Assistance

"I can't believe I went to rehearsal last night," Digby said. "And yet I missed all the drama."

"It was terrible," Nina said, shuddering. "I thought I was afraid of the dark before all that happened."

"Nina, would you help me with this batter?" Heather asked.

They were in the Donut Delights kitchen, and she hoped that having her assistant focus on a task she enjoyed would help her forget about the horrors of the night before.

"I can't believe someone famous died right down the street," Digby said, as he sliced up some pineapple for the recipe. "I know Art Sandford wasn't as big as he used to be, but people still knew his name."

"I'm going to be sleeping with the lights on for a few days. I can tell you that," Nina said, stirring more frantically than usual. "If I had known there was a killer on the loose, I never would have taken my seat."

A thought occurred to Heather. "Nina, you were seated further back than I was."

"I hope you don't think I was avoiding you. It wasn't that I didn't want to sit near you. But you already looked like you had a group of friends already."

"I didn't think that, though you are always welcome to sit with me."

"I was working up the courage to sit near the guy who works at Sun and Fun Novelties, but then I lost my nerve and sat in the back."

"It's because you were sitting there that I have a question. Did you notice anyone rushing past you after the lights went out?"

Nina thought about it even though it was clear that this was something she would rather forget. "There was movement, but it was more fearful and confused. No one ran past me with a purpose. I think I would have registered that because my sensors were on high alert. Is that helpful?"

"Very," Heather told her. "It confirms that the shooter needed to be someone from the front of the room. I'm going to discount Eva and Leila as suspects."

"They might be fiery, but I can't see those nice old ladies killing anyone," Digby agreed.

"So that means that it had to be either one of the writers or their guests that were seated up front," said Heather.

"I like thinking that I was helpful," said Nina. "But if it's something as important as that, maybe you should check with Janae too."

"That's a good idea. Could you two finish up these donuts?"

Her assistants agreed, and she left them to create their confectionary magic. Janae finished serving a customer as Heather came to the front of the shop to see her.

"How's the case coming?" Janae asked. "Do you think you'll be able to solve it faster because you were there?"

"I wish," Heather said.

She asked the same question that she had asked Nina and was given a similar answer.

"No. I didn't notice anyone rushing towards the writers. Are you trying to determine where the killer came from?"

"Exactly and it looks like they had to be in front of us."

Janae started putting a donut on a plate, and Heather looked around for a reason. Amy was about to walk through the door. Heather smiled. This only further proved how good Janae was at paying attention to her surroundings.

Amy accepted the donut and recapped her morning. "Jamie has taken over the task of rereading all of Art Sandford's books. He'll see if there are any references to industrialists or if the clues match up from his book."

"Tell him I really appreciate it, but I suspect there won't be any. I think Art Sandford was trying to prove that he could come up with a new story idea."

Then, Heather updated her partner on what she had learned from her assistants in the audience.

The Donut Delights' door swung open again, but this time Janae didn't prepare a donut plate. Instead, she bit her lip as she saw Fire Frank and Detective Peters enter the shop together.

"Why do they always get the same lunchbreaks?" Amy muttered.

"Hi Janae, I'm really sorry about yesterday. I didn't want to leave you at the panel," Detective Peters said. "But I had to investigate the call."

"I understand," Janae said. "You're a police officer, and you need to do your job. It's the same with Fire Frank. You two are never quite sure when you'll be called to do your duty."

"I'm glad you understand," Peters said. "But I still feel really bad about leaving you. First, I felt bad just because I wanted to spend time with you. But now knowing that I left you when there was a killer nearby? Well, now I feel truly awful."

"I took care of her," Fire Frank said. "I mean, as a friend. And not that she couldn't take care of herself. Because I know how strong and capable of handling herself she is."

Janae giggled. "You two are both really cute. I'm sorry that this situation is so awkward."

"I'd rather it be awkward with you than not-awkward without you," Fire Frank said. "And Peters is a good guy. It's good that we're becoming friends."

"Yes," Peters said. "I guess I feel bad about leaving you with the killer as well. And it ended up being a bust too. The call we got about a dead body turned out just to be some driftwood. And it took us away from where an actual crime was happening. What are the odds?"

"What are the odds, indeed?" Heather asked, officially joining their conversation. "Peters, do you think it's possible that the killer made that call to get you and Ryan away from the panel?"

"I hadn't thought of it before," Peters said. "But that could have been what happened. That means this murder was definitely premeditated."

"Could you trace the call and see who placed it?" asked Heather.

"Sure," said Peters. "But, you mean right now?"

"There is a killer on the loose," Heather reminded.

"I'll see you later, Janae," he said, trying not to sound disappointed. "I must away when duty calls."

He left, and Fire Frank ordered a Pineapple Cream Donut.

"I know that I should associate them with the murder and not want any," he said. "But they're just too delicious."

Heather and Amy wandered away from the counter, discussing the implications of the killer calling the police away from the soon-to-be crime scene. This killer was smart and had planned out the execution perfectly.

"Look," Heather said, changing the topic abruptly. "Isn't that Patterson Blake out there?"

"What's he doing? Besides looking suspicious in those dark clothes and sunglasses?"

"Let's find out," Heather said, heading out the door.

Chapter 11 – A Suspicious Character

"I've wanted to speak with you," Patterson Blake said as they approached. Heather and Amy paused.

"What do you mean?" Amy asked. "We came out to talk to you."

"I knew you wouldn't be able to resist," Patterson Blake said. "I heard that you were the real crime solvers on the island."

"Were you spying on us?" Heather asked.

"Don't be ridiculous," Patterson said. "The characters in my novels are spies. Not me."

He stared at them from behind his dark glasses and leaned against the wall.

"Then who have you been talking to?" asked Heather.

"I noticed how the police chief trusted you the night of the incident. And then I've heard stories on the island. A reporter wanted to quote me about what happened. She was very persistent."

"That must be Hope," Heather said, remembering her own

unwanted interviews with the young, driven reporter.

"She mentioned how you solved several murders around the island and one on a cruise ship."

"And that's just since we moved here," Amy said, proudly.

"I assume that now you're going to solve this case."

"We're assisting the police," said Heather. "We're licensed private investigators."

"As well as bakers?" he asked with a smile.

"Why did you want to talk to us?" Heather asked, crossing her arm. She was tired of playing games.

"You like to get directly to the point, don't you? I wanted to talk to you because I assume you're making a suspect list of who would want to kill Art Sandford. I also assumed that I would be on it, and I'd like to be removed."

"What makes you think you're on it?" asked Heather.

"This murder was cleverly planned to leave us all wondering which of the many people in the room could have pulled the trigger, and it was coolly executed to happen at precisely the right time. These are the hallmarks of all the murderers in my books. Of course, you would consider their creator to be a suspect."

"What about your motive?" asked Heather.

"Not as strong as others."

"We heard that Art Sandford didn't want to sit next to you at the panel," said Amy.

Patterson Blake shook his head. "Art Sandford had a problem with me more than I had a problem with him. I was the next generation of writer, and he wasn't ready to step aside. He

hadn't published anything in
years, so I didn't see him as a
real threat. I don't believe those
sentiments were mutual."

"He thought you were replacing
him?" asked Heather.

"And in a sense, I was. Readers
were flocking to my thrillers after
he stopped releasing books.
However, if I do say so myself, I
don't think I was just a
replacement. I was the evolution
of the genre. He had the Sherlock
Holmes and Watson dynamic
where one character always talks
about how smart the other one is.
I just had one character
constantly escaping explosions
as he solved a mystery."

"You said that your motive wasn't as strong as others," said Heather. "Did you have another suspect in mind?"

"It's always possible that it was a deranged fan," Patterson Blake admitted. "But I think it was more likely that it was someone who knew Art Sandford. And no one knew him better than Jess Krueger."

"Dennis Grimm's manager?" asked Amy.

"That's right," Patterson agreed. "She used to be Art Sandford's manager too."

"Why isn't she anymore?" asked Heather.

"I don't know the specifics. But I know there was bad blood between them. It took her a long time until she found another client again. She would be the number one suspect on my list."

"Except that she wasn't at the bookshop during the panel discussion," Heather said.

"She wasn't? I saw her there earlier in the day. Wasn't she there to watch Dennis Grimm talk on the panel? She was obsessing over his comfort all day."

"She arrived after the murder because she was taking an important phone call."

"I see," Patterson Blake said, not expecting to be contradicted. "Maybe she had Dennis Grimm pull the trigger for her."

"We can talk to him about that. He's the one writer that we haven't spoken to yet."

"Good luck," Patterson Blake said, dramatically.

Heather sensed that what he said would have been the last line in one of his chapters with the lead spy staring off into the distance.

Heather and Amy shuffled away awkwardly. Then, they began walking down the street processing everything that they had just learned.

"Heather, I'm not a Watson, am I?"

"If by Watson, you mean an invaluable partner who solves cases with me, then you might be. I couldn't solve these cases without you."

"I'm not just someone who says how smart you are?"

"Nope. You pull your own weight. And I know you love me, but you're honest, and you keep me from getting a big head. The only thing you ever consistently praise is my donuts."

"Well, if you ever did make a bad one, I'd tell you."

They two women laughed until they realized that their walking had led them over to Bernadette's Beachy Books. They saw someone sneak behind the building and they stopped in their tracks.

"I better call Ryan about this."

"I hope it's not Lori Laurels investigating again."

"It didn't look like Lori," Heather said. "But there's a good chance it could be the killer."

Chapter 12 – The Mysterious Stranger

Heather and Amy kept their distance as they followed the stranger. They didn't want him to know they were there, but they also wanted to make sure that potentially important evidence wasn't destroyed at the crime scene.

"Do you recognize him?" Heather asked.

"No," Amy said. "I don't know him from around town. And I don't think I saw him at the writers' panel the night of the murder."

"But if he wasn't at the event and he couldn't be the killer, then what is he doing here?"

He just seemed to be looking around. He kept checking his phone and walking around the premise. Then, he tried to open the back door.

Heather rushed forward. "What are you doing?"

"What are *you* doing?" Amy asked. "I thought we were waiting for backup."

"Ryan is on his way," Heather said, turning back to her friend. "And we can't let him disrupt the scene."

"But—"

"If he wasn't inside the bookshop, then he can't be the killer."

"That doesn't mean he's not dangerous," Amy retorted.

The man walked over to meet them. "Are one of you Bernadette?"

"No, but we're friends of hers. I own the donut shop down the street. Why are you looking for her?"

"I'm Fritz. I'm from Appliances of the Fritz. I'm a repairman. She hired me to fix her air conditioner."

"With all the excitement, she must have forgotten to cancel," Heather said.

"I saw the caution tape, but I didn't know if this was a real crime scene or not. When Bernadette called me about the air conditioner going out, she mentioned she was having some sort of detective event. She was really upset, but this was the earliest I could come. I don't normally work Sundays, and I couldn't get out of my plans to help her out. That's why I've been walking around looking for her. Is it a real crime scene though?"

"It is," Heather said. "One of the mystery writers was murdered."

"I hope the air conditioner not working didn't contribute to it," Fritz said.

"I don't believe so," Heather said with a smile.

"I guess I should be going then if it's all roped off for real."

"Why don't you stick around for a little while? The lead investigator will be here any minute. He can tell you if fixing the air conditioner will affect the scene or not. I'm sure it would be some comfort to Bernadette to know that one problem was taken care of."

Fritz agreed to wait for a little while, but he spent the time selling them on his business. By the time Ryan arrived, Heather was ready to call him to fix any of her appliances that started giving her trouble.

Ryan noticed how calm everyone was as he approached and breathed a sigh of relief.

"He's not the killer," Heather explained. "He's the air conditioner repairman."

"I still wish you had waited for me to arrive," Ryan said. "But I'm glad this was a false alarm."

Ryan allowed Fritz to enter the bookshop and decided that

repairing the system wouldn't
damage the scene in any way.

"I'll just have to keep an eye on
the repairs and on you while
you're inside the building," Ryan
explained.

"No problem at all," Fritz replied.

He started setting up his supplies
by the air conditioner, and Ryan
found a comfortable spot where
he would be able to see
everything.

"Thanks for letting this get fixed,"
Heather said.

"I'm happy that we can do
something for the bookshop. I

feel like I haven't made much progress with the case. I visited Art Sandford's room at the bed and breakfast, and there wasn't anything helpful there. He didn't keep any more clues to the fake murder in his room, and there wasn't anything to indicate that he was feuding with anyone."

"Amy and I were going to find Dennis Grimm and talk with him. He's the only writer we haven't spoken to yet."

"Hello?" a voice called out, interrupting them. "Is anyone there?"

"Gina?" Heather asked, recognizing the dark hair as she entered.

"Hi," Bernadette's assistant said. "I wanted to make sure that it was someone who was supposed to be here who was inside."

"What are you doing here?" asked Heather.

"Bernadette has been pretty distraught since this all happened. I didn't think that she remembered to cancel the repairman, but I didn't know who she had called to come in, so I couldn't actually call him back. I thought I'd come and apologize for wasting his time, though they were unusual circumstances. But now it seems like I don't have to. You let him in to fix things?"

Heather nodded.

"Officer," Fritz called, waving Ryan over. "I think there's something that you're going to want to see."

The others followed right behind the detective so they could see too.

"Um… what are we looking at?" asked Amy.

"This repair isn't because something wore out or was

shorted," Fritz explained. "These parts here have been cut."

"Deliberately?" asked Ryan.

"I would say so," Fritz said. "Why would somebody do that?"

Heather considered the question. Was it possible that the air conditioner was sabotaged for a reason? Could it have something to do with the murder? But if so, was it part of Art Sandford's pretend murder game? Or was it part of the killer's plot?

"Stop repairing for now," Ryan said. "I'll start taking some fingerprints in case it relates to the murder."

"But how could it relate?" asked Amy. "Could the gun have been hidden in there until the killer needed it?"

"I don't know," Heather said. "But I do know that we have one more writer suspect that I want to talk to."

Ryan promised to keep them updated on his end, while Heather and Amy set out to question Dennis Grimm.

Chapter 13 – Dennis Grimm

"My client has already spoken to the police. I don't know why he has to talk to you."

"Calm down, Jess," Dennis said. "You're making it sound like you're my lawyer and you're my manager."

"I'm still looking out for your well-being."

"It's all right," Dennis said. "They just want to find out what happened to Art Sandford. And I do too."

Dennis admitted Heather and Amy into his room at the bed and breakfast. It featured the cozy décor of most bed and breakfast rooms but also had some cardboard cutouts of werewolves that he must have used during his time at the book signing table.

"I don't know how you could sleep with those wolves staring at you," Amy commented.

"At this point, Wes Wolfe is one of my best friends. Maybe an imaginary friend. But he feels real on the pages," Dennis said. "But, I'm sorry. Let's get back to the case at hand."

"Yes," Heather said. "We'd like to know more about your movements during the shooting."

"It's funny," Dennis said. "I've done a lot shooting before. As research for my books. Silver bullets are an important part of them. And I feel like I didn't have a quick reaction to the first shot. It sounded fake to me."

"That might have been a recording," Heather said.

"The second shot sounded real. I jumped out of my seat and then crouched down. I wasn't sure where it was coming from."

"That's the natural reaction for any human being," Jess said.

"But you didn't move from the general location of your seat?" Heather asked.

"No," Jess said. "And he didn't run around shoot Art Sandford."

"I stayed by my seat," Dennis said more calmly.

"And did you notice if anyone else moved?"

"I was on the other end of the line of chairs," Dennis said. "And it was very dark. I would only have noticed Lori Laurels moving. It seemed like she hid behind her chair."

"And where were you at the time of the murder?" Heather asked Jess Krueger.

"I was on an important call with a publisher. I told you this before."

"Yes, but where were you physically?"

"Oh, I see. I was wandering around outside of our accommodations. The weather was so nice, and I wanted to be able to head over to the Mystery Writers' Panel as soon as I was finished on the phone."

"Did anyone see you?"

"I don't know."

Amy was taking notes on her tablet, as Heather changed gears in her questioning.

"How well did you two know Art Sandford?"

"I never met him before this event," Dennis said. "I was familiar with his work, but I didn't know him as a person."

"Did he mention anything to you about something he might have had planned for the event?"

"No," Dennis said, raising an eyebrow. "But if you said that the first gunshot was recorded, then I would guess that he had a murder game planned. Did he want the other writers to solve the case?"

"That seems like a possibility," said Heather.

"He didn't tell me what he had planned, but he did wink at me when he said that the discussion tonight would be interesting. At the time, I thought that he was referring to me being a young writer and I should be prepared for the stories I would hear. Now it makes more sense if he were planning a challenge for us. But how did it turn into a real murder?"

"That's what we've been trying to figure out," Amy muttered.

"Ms. Krueger, did you know about Art Sandford's plan?" Heather asked.

"I suppose I knew he was up to something with his assistant based on the way they were acting, but I didn't think anything of it. I didn't know exactly what they planned. Frankly, I didn't care. My main focus was taking care of Dennis."

"We heard that you took good care of him through the day. You were very particular about certain things."

"I had to look out for him. He's my client. And it was stifling at the bookshop that day."

"She's a great manager," Dennis said. "My Wes Wolfe books have really taken off since she took me on."

"We heard that there was a bit of a hiatus between you having any clients," Heather said. "Was there a particular reason?"

"I was waiting for the right one. Someone who had the potential to make it big."

"Aw. Thanks, Jess," Dennis said.

"And your client before this was Art Sandford?"

Jess Krueger bristled at the memory. "Yes. That's right. And it wasn't a good relationship. But I didn't kill him. I wasn't there."

"Why was it a bad relationship?" Heather prompted.

"Because he didn't want to listen to my advice. I'm always looking out for the best interests of my clients. He ignored what I had to say and then fired me. And look what he's done without me? Nothing. Not a book since then."

"You don't seem particularly upset about his death," Heather said.

"I am upset. I'm upset that he was killed. And I'm upset that you keep questioning Dennis. You can't possibly think that he had anything to do with it."

"We believe it was one of the writers or their guests who sat up front that committed the crime."

"But why would it be Dennis? He didn't know him."

"Maybe he was helping his beloved manager get rid of someone that she hated?" Amy suggested.

"That's ridiculous," Jess said, getting upset.

"We do know that the murderer was a good shooter," said Heather. "He needed to hit one particular person in a darkened room."

"I've only shot targets before. As research," said Dennis. "I've never hurt anyone."

"Once we find the murder weapon, I'm sure we can determine more about who could have used it," Heather said.

"Why are you wasting your time talking to us?" Jess asked. "We didn't have anything to do with this. But you know who could have? Lori Laurels. She was going on about how bad Art Sandford had been when they dated."

"She did say that Art Sandford didn't respect her work," Dennis admitted.

"That sounds like a motive to me," Jess said.

"Yes, but this isn't one of the werewolf mysteries," Amy said. "We need evidence to back up any suspicions we had."

"And I think we'll go continue to search for that evidence," Heather said. "Thank you for answering our questions."

Chapter 14 – Who Knew?

Heather set the table, disappointed that no new evidence had come to light after she left Dennis Grimm's room. Ryan told her that no fingerprints had turned up on the air conditioner. It also seemed like any cutting tool could have done the trick, so there was no way to rule people out for the sabotage.

Gina couldn't remember anyone by the air conditioner that morning until Bernadette checked it out when the writers were complaining that it was hot. However, it was possible that someone could have snuck back there without her noticing and committed the deed. She was more focused on fixing the wires for the podcast. All the writers had access to the building and could have done it, including Art Sandford himself.

"Do you need any help, Mom?" Lilly asked, joining her at the kitchen table.

"Only protecting me from these hungry animals," Heather teased.

Her white dog, Dave, and kitten, Cupcake, were staying underfoot in the hopes that Heather would spill some dinner or donuts on the floor. Lilly giggled and picked Cupcake up to get her out of the way.

When the table was set, they both sat down, waiting for Ryan to join them.

"Are you doing all right, honey?" Heather asked her daughter.

"Yes. I know what happened was really bad, and it was scary at the time, but something good actually did come out of it. I really liked hanging out with Chelsea, and I think we're going to become friends. And I think it's always good if you can try and find something positive in a situation."

"Those are wise words," Heather said. "And I'd love to invite Chelsea to come over for a playdate."

"Will you make donuts?"

"Of course!"

Dave and Cupcake danced around at the sound of the word "donuts." Ryan entered and watched them bounce around.

"Somehow I don't think this enthusiasm is for me."

"They love you," Heather said. "But we were just talking about donuts."

"I guess I can't compete with that."

They had a nice family meal together, and Heather felt happier

171

than she had since the case began. She felt better knowing that Lilly was going to be all right, and had even made a friend.

It was after Lilly went to bed that Heather began to focus on the case again. It wasn't adding up correctly. It was as if three writers plus a sister minus a manager and a missing gun somehow equaled murder.

She sat on the couch and scratched Dave's tummy.

"Do you want a late-night snack?" Ryan asked, entering the room with two of her Pineapple Cream Donuts.

"Of course I do," Heather said. "But you've made a tactical error asking me in front of Dave."

"I suppose he can have a little bit since he's such a good boy."

Dave wagged his tail.

The humans were quiet as they enjoyed their donuts. Then, Ryan turned to his wife and asked, "Are you thinking about the case?"

"I'm thinking about how I'd like to solve it to help Bernadette. But there are so many suspects, and they all seem adept at planning complicated crimes. And this one is certainly complicated."

"Part of the problem seems to be separating Art Sandford's fake murder plot from the actual murder."

"I wish the real killer had left labeled clues around the scene," Heather joked.

"That would make it easier." Ryan laughed.

"Wait a second," Heather said. "We were joking, but it's actually given me an idea."

"Are those labeled clues more helpful than we thought?"

"No. I don't think so. Jamie has been reading the author's crime books to make sure that we're not missing a reference. But that's not what I was referring to."

"What have you come up with?"

"The killer plotted out this crime. He called in a report of a dead body to get the police on the other side of the island when this murder took place."

"And unfortunately, Peters wasn't able to trace the call back to the caller."

"The killer needed the room to be dark and for there to be enough confusion to get away with this. I think the killer knew about Art

Sandford's idea for a fake murder and used their knowledge to plan their own crime. It was the perfect cover."

"That makes sense," Ryan agreed. "So, who knew about Art Sandford's plan?"

"From my interviews, it seems like lots of people were suspicious about what Art Sandford was up to, but they didn't know the specifics."

"Or they didn't want to admit that they knew what the plan was?" Ryan suggested. "Because they knew it might at some point relate back to their guilt."

"That could be it too," Heather agreed. "We need to find out exactly who knew about the plan. And I know who we need to talk to about that."

***

"I don't like being back here again," Connor Johnson said as he sat down at the interrogation table.

"I don't like it either," Amy said. "It means that we didn't get all the information we needed the first time around."

"I tried to tell you everything," Connor said.

The four investigators looked at him. He was less sweaty than the last time they had met him, though he still looked like he hadn't gotten much rest.

"We need to know everyone who knew about Art Sandford's plan for the fake murder," said Heather.

"Why do you need to know that?" asked Connor.

"Because we believe the person who knew about his plan used it to cover their own murder plan. One that was successful in killing the writer," said Heather.

"And right now, the only person we know for sure who knew about the plan was you," said Ryan.

"I didn't kill him!" Connor said.

"You knew about his plan," Detective Peters said.

"Yes. But I told you that so you'd know that I didn't know about the real murder."

"Did you follow that?" asked Amy.

"I only knew about the fake murder. I didn't know about the real one. And I thought for a while that Mr. Sandford had killed himself as a stunt."

179

"He didn't," Ryan said. "He couldn't have shot himself in the way he did."

"Poor guy," Connor said. "He really was a good boss then."

"Who else knew?" asked Heather.

"I don't think Art Sandford told anyone besides me."

"And who did you tell?" asked Ryan.

"All right. Fine. I'll tell you," Connor said. "I was trying to impress Lana Laurels, the writer's sister. I thought she was really pretty and she didn't have the time of day for me, so I told her about the plan to try and impress her. It didn't work... She's the only one I told."

"But that doesn't mean that she's the only one who knew," Heather said. "If Lana Laurels knew about the plan, there's a good chance that Lori Laurels knew about it too."

"The ex-girlfriend just became our prime suspect," said Amy.

Chapter 15 – The Sisters

"This is nothing like how I describe it in my books," Lori Laurels said.

She and her sister were seated at the table in the interrogation room. Heather, Amy, and Ryan sat across from them.

Detective Peters had been called away to answer another anonymous call. This time it was about an abandoned weapon. He decided that he could check it out on his own so that there was no delay in questioning the Laurels sisters.

"It's a little like your books," Lana said, kittenishly. "The detective here is pretty handsome."

"I think he's also married to one of the P.I.s, so saying that isn't going to help us get out of trouble."

"I don't understand why we are in trouble," Lana protested. "We didn't have anything to do with that writer's death."

"But your sister did date him," Ryan said.

"And, I know, it was a terrible decision. But it wasn't so bad that I wanted to kill him," Lori said.

"Even if he didn't take your work seriously?" asked Amy.

"If she killed everyone who didn't take her books seriously, she wouldn't have time to do anything except kill critics," Lana said.

"Hey!"

"It's true."

"It's still hurtful."

"I love your books, sis. And you have lots of fans. But not everyone appreciates them."

"Art Sandford was one of those people," Lori admitted. "But I didn't kill him."

"Lana, we'd like to talk to you about a conversation you had with Connor Johnson," said Heather.

"Who?"

"Art Sandford's assistant."

"Who?"

"Come on," Lori said. "That kid who was helping Art get set up. He was trying to impress you."

"Right. I guess I kind of remember him."

"He told you about Art Sandford's plan for the mystery game that

night, didn't he?" Heather
prompted.

"I guess that's what he was going
on about," said Lana. "I was
trying to find a polite way to leave
the conversation. I wasn't really
paying attention to what he was
saying."

"We believe that somebody who
knew about Art Sandford's plan
for the fake murder is the
murderer," said Ryan.

"But I didn't know about it!" Lana
protested. "Not really. I wasn't
paying attention to him."

"I'm always telling her that she should pay more attention to people," Lori said.

"I don't know," Amy said. "It seems pretty convenient that she was told the perfect time to murder someone and wasn't paying attention."

"But I wasn't," Lana said.

"And just because he told her doesn't mean that she was the only one who knew," Lori said. "There were people walking around the bookstore all morning while things were being set up. Anyone could have overheard what he was telling her."

"Like who?" asked Heather.

"Well, Patterson Blake was skulking around like a spy. And Jess Krueger was making demands for Dennis Grimm. Any of them could have overheard the plan. And maybe the assistant was the killer all along. Did you ever think of that?"

"Yes," Heather said. "But it doesn't seem very likely."

"Well, it's always the person you least suspect," said Lori.

"Have you ever fired a gun before?" Ryan asked, changing the subject.

"Never," said Lana.

"I've fired before on a range, trying to learn about it for my books. I wouldn't say that I'm really great at it. I don't have perfect aim. And I wouldn't have trusted myself to fire at a particular target in a crowd."

"Lana, where were you when all this was going on?" asked Heather.

"I was frozen in fear," Lana said. "I didn't know what to do. I wanted to help Lori, but I couldn't see. I just froze."

Ryan's phone rang.

"It's Peters," he said. He gestured for Heather and Amy to follow him out of the interrogation room so he could update them on any developments his partner might have. When he hung up, he told them quickly. "This anonymous call wasn't the dud that the last one turned out to be."

"The weapon wasn't driftwood?" Amy asked.

"No," Ryan said. "It's the same caliber as the murder weapon. And it looks to be the same make and model of Art Sandford's gun. He's going to doublecheck the serial numbers when he gets back."

"It sounds like he found the murder weapon," Heather said.

"And that's not all," said Ryan. "This might be our biggest break yet. There was a hair stuck to it."

"A hair?" asked Amy.

"A long dark strand of hair," Ryan said.

The trio turned to look through the two-way mirror at the Laurels sisters with their matching dark hair.

Chapter 16 – The Hair

Waiting for the result of the DNA test for the hair found on the gun felt like an eternity, even though Heather knew that they were getting the results rushed. In the time it took to receive the results, they had already determined that the gun that Detective Peters had found was indeed the murder weapon.

However, they had not gotten either of the Laurels sisters to confess to their involvement in the murder.

Heather cleaned the glass display at Donut Delights, thinking about her case. Why did Art Sandford bring his gun to Key

192

West? Was it supposed to have been part of his murder game? Wouldn't that have been dangerous? How did the Laurels sisters get the gun away from him? And, most importantly, which of the sisters was the one to pull the trigger?

Heather phone rang, and she answered it immediately.

"Are you sitting down?" Ryan asked.

"I'm leaning on the donut counter," Heather said. "But I can take it. I'm guessing you have the results of the DNA test. Who did the hair belong to? Lori or Lana?"

"Neither," Ryan said. "It belonged to Bernadette's assistant, Gina."

"Gina?"

"That's right. I'm going to have to pick her up now."

"But why would Gina have killed him?"

"We can question her and see if we can get some answers."

"But it doesn't make any sense," Heather protested.

"That's the results of the DNA test," Ryan said. "Her hair was stuck was the one stuck on the gun."

"I guess I'll see you at the station," Heather said. "I'll bring some donuts over."

She hung up unhappily. If this were true, it would kill Bernadette. Gina had been her assistant for years. She had always been a good worker and a friend to her, and she had never shown any murderous tendencies before.

Heather boxed up some Pineapple Cream Donuts to bring with her. She needed to get to the station and figure out what was going on.

***

"I've never used a gun before, and I certainly didn't use one to kill a famous writer who I was trying to record during a podcast," Gina said.

"Your hair was found stuck to the gun," Ryan said. "Can you explain that?"

"No," Gina said. "But I didn't kill anyone."

"Did you handle a gun as a prop for the event?" Heather asked.

It was strange seeing Gina in the interrogation room. Heather kept looking for ways to prove that it wasn't the assistant who had committed the murder. She told herself to remain objective but also reminded herself that she was a good judge of character. She was sure that Gina wasn't the killer. But, then, how did her hair end up on the murder weapon?

"No," Gina said. "Bernadette wouldn't have wanted them in the shop. And this was just supposed to be a discussion. There wasn't supposed to be a murder or a fake murder like you're saying took place."

"You didn't know anything about Art Sandford's plan that night?" Detective Peters asked.

"No. I would have stopped him if I knew. It could have ruined the whole night. Well, it did ruin the whole night, but not in the way he thought," said Gina. "And I wasn't at the bookshop the entire morning. I needed to buy new cables because I needed to be able to record the discussion."

"You did help with setting up the event," Ryan said. "So, you knew where everyone would be."

"Yes, but I didn't kill anyone. Can I please go home?"

"I'm sorry," said Ryan. "But right now all the evidence is pointing to you. We're going to have to hold you."

"But it's Gina," Amy said. "Do you really think she did it?"

"Are you asking me to ignore a suspect's DNA on a murder weapon?" Ryan asked. "I don't like this any better than you do, but we can't let our personal feelings cloud our judgment."

"Her fingerprints weren't on the gun," Heather pointed out.

"She must have wiped down the gun," Ryan said. "That could have been when her hair got stuck on it because she was in a rush when she disposed of it."

"It's okay," Gina said to Heather. "I know you have to do your jobs.

199

But I also know that you'll keep digging until you find the real killer."

"I will," Heather promised.

"Can I ask you a favor?"

"Besides having us find the real murderer to set you free?" asked Amy.

"Could you finish editing the podcast?" Gina asked. "I sent it to myself as it was recording, so I had a copy. I'm only going to air it if it's tasteful, but mystery fans have been asking to hear it. I'd obviously cut it before the shooting starts, but if Art Sandford's answers to the questions are good – this might be a nice tribute to him. Could you listen to it and see?"

Heather agreed. She wasn't sure how skilled she would be with editing, but she was anxious to hear what had been recorded that night. She hadn't thought much about it at the time because she had been at the scene when the murder took place. However, it was possible that the microphones had picked up something useful that she hadn't noticed at the time.

***

"This is weird," Amy said. "Listening to the discussion again when you know someone is about to die during it."

The two friends were in Amy's house so Jamie could help them if they had any technological problems. He had been trying to become more tech-savvy, and he was hoping he could help with the case because reading Art Sandford's books hadn't revealed any clues to him.

"I can see Gina's dilemma about releasing it," Heather said. "If she doesn't, then Art Sanford's last words about his craft won't be heard by his fans. However, they were his last words."

"Creepy," Amy agreed.

They listened to the recording knowing that the gunshots would come soon.

"I like to begin with a red herring or a misled," Art Sandford's voice proclaimed.

"Wait," Heather said. "Go back."

"Are you sure?" Amy asked. "This is creepy enough."

"I have to agree with Amy on this one," said Jamie.

"I think I heard something," Heather said.

"Gunshots?" Amy asked.

"No," Heather said, rolling her eyes. "Can you please play it back? I think I heard something after he said red herring."

Jamie dutifully played the section back.

"Do you hear it?" Heather asked.

"It sounds like a popping sound," Jamie said.

He played it again, and they all heard it: Pop. Pop.

"Oh my goodness," Amy said. "Is that noise what I think it is?"

Heather nodded. "And that means I think I just solved the case."

Chapter 17 – The Perfect Murder

"I'm very nervous about this," Bernadette said.

"Don't worry," said Heather. "We're all right here as back up. And doing this will clear Gina's name, and save your business, and catch a killer."

"I know the reasons," Bernadette said. "That's why I agreed to do this. Still, I can't help but feel like I'm headed to the guillotine like in *A Tale of Two Cities*."

The door to Bernadette's Beachy Books opened. Heather hid out of sight with Amy and Ryan, as Bernadette faced her visitor.

"This seems like a strange place
to meet," Jess Krueger said.

"I still have the keys to my shop,"
Bernadette said. "And I didn't
want to invite a killer to my
home."

"You said that you have
something that I'd want to buy?
I'm listening," Jess Krueger said.

"I have the file from what we
recorded the night of the murder
for the podcast. There's
something to give you away."

"What?"

"You were outside the bookshop
when you fired. That was smart.

We didn't suspect it. But you stepped on something outside the window when you got into position to shoot. Bubble wrap. You can hear it popping on the recording. And there was no bubble wrap inside the room. Only outside."

"That doesn't prove I killed him."

"Fine," Bernadette said. "I thought this was a nice time to make a deal. I could use some money now that my bookstore is ruined. But I could turn this over to the police and let them deal with the implications of the murderer being outside."

"No," Jess Krueger said. "I'm interested. I want to make a deal."

"Did you bring the cash?"

"It's in my bag," she said, moving slowly closer.

"But why did you kill him in my shop?" Bernadette asked.

"I killed him because he fired me. I'd been waiting for the right opportunity to get him back. Your shop just provided the opportunity," said Jess. "Of course, I'm going to kill you in your shop for another reason. To close your big mouth."

She advanced on Bernadette whose eyes widened with fear. Ryan emerged from his hiding place in a flash.

"Freeze right there," Ryan said.

"Officer, I'm so glad you're here," Jess said. "This woman was trying to extort me."

Heather and Amy joined the group.

"Nice try," Amy said. "But we were recording this conversation too."

Jess Krueger put her purse down. "How did you know?"

"Like Bernadette said when we heard the popping sound, we realized that the killer was actually outside the window," said Heather.

"For once my littering actually helped," Amy joked

"Because of the close range, we thought that it had to be someone inside the room," said Heather. "But if you were right outside the window, it would have the same effect."

"That's why you broke my air conditioner," Bernadette said. "And why you kept making such a racket about it being too hot for your client. You needed to make sure that the windows would be open during the discussion when you wanted to kill him."

"You must have overheard Connor Johnson trying to impress Lana by telling her about Art Sandford's mystery game. You decided that would be the perfect time to attack," Heather continued.

"I took his gun when I was still his manager. I've been holding onto it for years, waiting for the right moment to use it on him. I wasn't sure that I was going to here, but I brought it just in case," Jess said. "And do you know what he said to me when he saw me? No hard feelings! That's what he said. Well, I did have hard feelings, and I decided to show him so."

"And you were the one who made the anonymous phone calls to get us far away from the writers and so we would find the murder weapon," said Ryan.

"That's right."

"The only thing I don't understand is why you tried to frame Gina of all people," Heather said. "We never considered her a serious suspect."

"I thought I was framing Lori Laurels," Jess said. "I grabbed a dark hair when I was at the bookshop to save in case I needed to plant any evidence. I didn't know it belonged to the assistant. Lori's hair looks the same."

"But why frame anyone?"

"Because I was afraid that you were considering Dennis a suspect," Jess said. "And I couldn't have that. I really would do anything for my current clients."

Ryan placed handcuffs on her and started leading her to the door. However, Jess Krueger couldn't resist saying, "I gave them a run for their money, didn't I? Those mystery writers. Mine was pretty good, wasn't it? Had you guessing for a while. I came up with it all on my own."

Ryan led her to the police care. Bernadette sighed with relief when she was gone.

"This means Gina will be set free?"

"Exactly," said Heather. "And you'll be able to open up the shop again."

"Thank you both," Bernadette said. "You're good friends."

Chapter 18 – Friends

"This is my mom's donut shop," Lilly said proudly, showing her freckled friend around.

"My dad is a big fan of her donuts. He talks about them a lot," Chelsea said.

"I'll pack up a box of donuts that you can give to him when you get home," Heather said. "But first, let's get you both a snack."

She led the girls over to the donut display counter. Chelsea's eyes widened, and Lilly grinned.

"There are so many," Chelsea said. "How can you ever decide?"

Janae smiled over the counter at the girls.

"Well," Lilly explained. "You want to try whatever the flavor of the week is, and this week it's called a Pineapple Cream Donut."

"That sounds good."

"They're all good! And you just sort of pick from the regular yummy flavors until you find your favorite."

"Janae, why don't you make a mix of a dozen donuts and bring it to their table?" Heather suggested. "It's a celebration so we can go a little crazy."

"A dozen donuts - coming right up," Janae said.

Heather led the girls to a table and listened as they talked about Lilly's dinosaur detective stories and about the stories that Chelsea wrote that focused on crimefighting cats.

Janae brought the donuts over to the table and was so charmed by the girls' enthusiasm for the snacks that she didn't notice Detective Peters and Fire Frank coming into the shop.

"Hi Janae," Detective Peters said. "My case is closed so I don't expect to be called away again."

"And we were wondering if maybe we could plan another activity was friends," said Fire Frank. "One that hopefully doesn't include a murder."

They chatted about potential plans, and Janae thanked them for being so patient and supportive. She knew that they really were both good guys.

At Heather's table, the discussion turned to talk about the murder.

"My dad says that he's in charge of making sure that all sorts of cases get solved," Chelsea said. "Even scary ones like murder. I can't believe you were there when that happened."

219

"It was really scary and sad," Lilly said. "But if I wasn't there, I don't know when I would have met you. And I'm really glad I did."

"Me too," Chelsea said. "But still, if I were there, I wouldn't have been able to handle it. I would have screamed so loud."

Heather's mouth was full, so she couldn't protest as Chelsea decided to showcase what she meant and let out a blood-curdling scream.

They weren't any other customers in the shop to frighten at that time, but Janae jumped right into the air. Then, acting on instinct, she ran into Fire Frank's arms.

Realizing what happened, Janae laughed. "I'm sorry. After a murder happened down the street, I realize I'm jumpy."

"I don't mind," Fire Frank said, hugging her.

Detective Peters looked like he did mind and was feeling sad. "Yeah. Murders are a scary thing. And, you know, I think I better get out there and patrol and make sure that nothing bad is happening."

"I didn't mean anything by this," Janae said, taking a step away from Fire Frank.

"I think maybe you did," Peters said. "Subconsciously or whatever. Fire Frank is who you want. And that's fine. And I will still be friends with you. But I think now I'd really like to go and make sure that the town is safe."

Peters left the shop.

"I hope I didn't hurt him," Janae said. "I wasn't thinking."

"I know," Fire Frank said. "And we can still take things slow, but if you would maybe want to go to a movie Friday night, I'd like that a lot."

"I'd like that too," Janae said with a smile. "Maybe we can sneak some donuts inside as snacks."

The couple giggled, but Chelsea looked sheepish at the table.

"Did I do something wrong?" Chelsea asked Heather.

"Actually, I think you finally got things into motion."

Heather smiled as the girls ate their donuts, thinking they were well on their way to becoming best friends. She couldn't wait to update her own best friend about the romance that had finally been decided at her donut shop.

The End.

A letter from the Author

To each and every one of my Amazing readers: I hope you enjoyed this story as much as I enjoyed writing it. Let me know what you think by leaving a review!

Stay Curious,
Susan Gillard

Made in the USA
Columbia, SC
23 February 2023

12882991R00124